Always Twins

Teri Weidner

Holiday House / New York

For Olivia and Lily, with love

HOLIDAY HOUSE is registered in the U.S. Patent and Trademark Office.
Printed and Bound in October 2014 at Toppan Leefung, DongGuan City, China
The artwork was created with watercolor and colored pencils.
www.holidayhouse.com
First Edition
1 3 5 7 9 10 8 6 4 2

Library of Congress Cataloging-in-Publication Data
Weidner, Teri.
Always twins / by Teri Weidner. — First edition.
pages cm
Summary: Duck twins Lily and Olivia are alike in many ways, including their love
for each other, but they can also be very different.
ISBN 978-0-8234-3159-5 (hardcover)
[1. Twins—Fiction. 2. Sisters—Fiction. 3. Individuality—Fiction. 4. Ducks—Fiction.] I. Title.
PZ7.W425737Alw 2015
[E]—dc23
2013043575

Lily and Olivia are twins.
Wherever they go, they hear . . .

"You two are just alike!"

"Yes, we are!" says Olivia.
"Just alike," says Lily.

But . . .

Olivia likes to
jump in the mud,

quack at bugs,

and race everywhere.

Lily likes to make
daisy chains,

gaze at clouds,

and study everything.

Sometimes these pastimes . . .

don't mix well.

Lily shouts,
"Olivia, you should **stop** barging around!"

Olivia shouts,
"Lily, you should **start** barging around!"

Then a dragonfly says,
"You two are just alike," ...

and the twins get mad.

"No, we're not!" says Lily.

"Not one bit!" says Olivia.

Olivia looks for a place
where Lily would never go.
Not ever, ever.

Lily sits and fumes.
She does **not** look for Olivia.
Not at all.

After a while, though, Lily starts to feel lonely.

"Olivia?" she calls. "Olivia?"

It is very quiet.

Then she hears, "Lily?"

A voice comes from the leaves.
"I'm here, Lily!"

Lily looks up.
"Oh my! You are up really high, Olivia."

"I can't get down," says Olivia.
"Oh no," says Lily,
"then I'll have to come up."

Lily is scared, but she climbs up anyway.

"That was so brave, Lily!" says Olivia.
"Thank you, Olivia," says Lily.

"But how will we ever get down?" Olivia asks.

Lily steps carefully and says,
"Let me look."
"I'll look too," says Olivia.

Suddenly there is a loud crack!

"I've got you, Lily!" calls Olivia.
"I've got you, Olivia!" calls Lily.

Down, down the twins fall.

They hit the water with a **big** splash.

"Are you all right?" asks a frog.

"Yes!" sputters Lily.
"I think so!" gurgles Olivia.

The frog blinks.

"Wow, you two are just alike!"

"Sometimes we are . . . ," says Olivia.

"And sometimes we aren't," says Lily.

"But we're always twins," say Lily and Olivia.
"Always, always twins!"